For Rotem

OLIVER
and his
EGG

Paul Schmid

DISNEP · HYPERION BOOKS

NEW YORK

When Oliver found his egg . . .

Oliver imagined

he had a friend

and they would grow

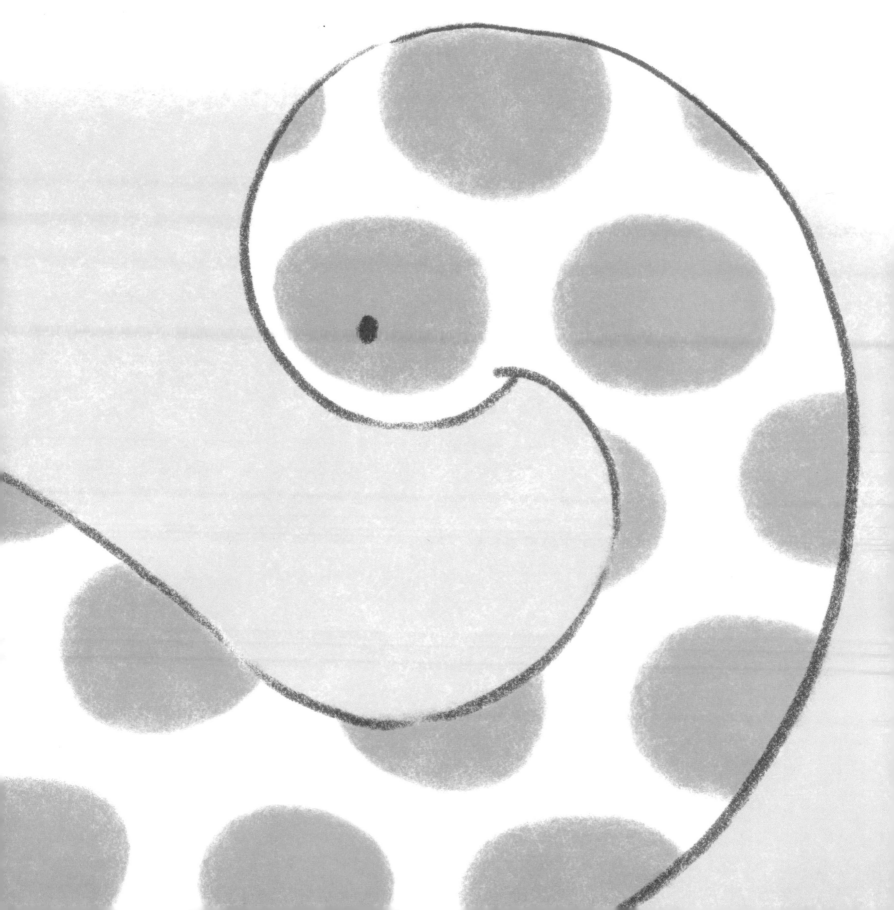

to have adventures,

and discover new worlds . . .

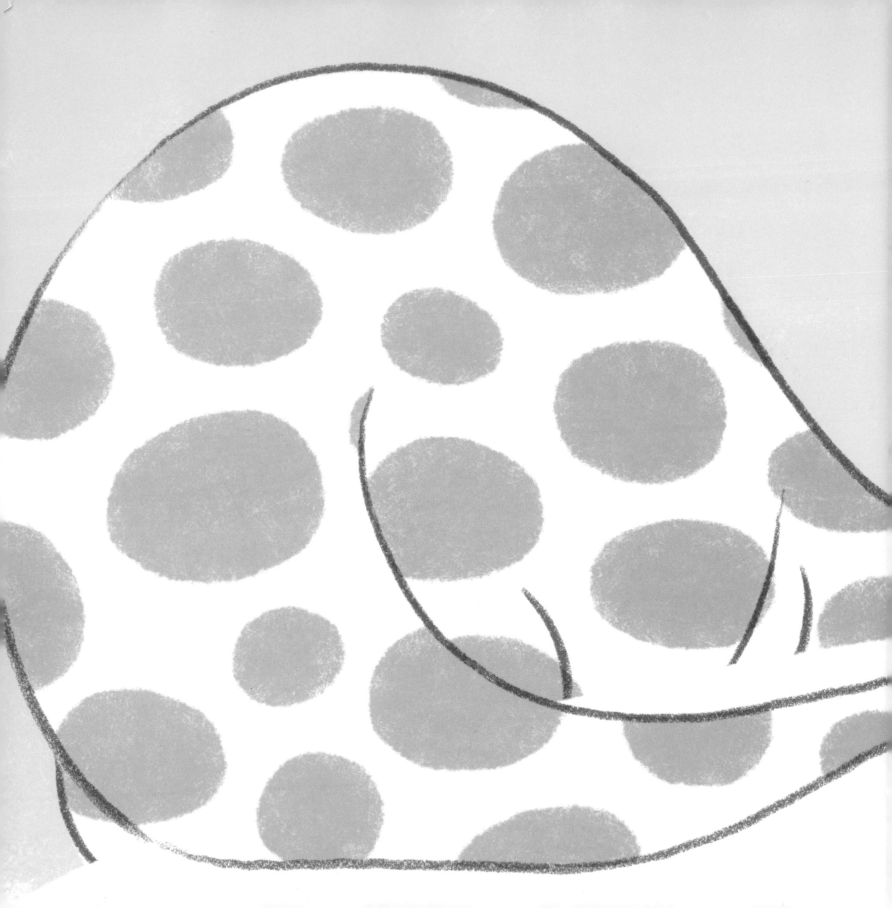

just the two of them

together.

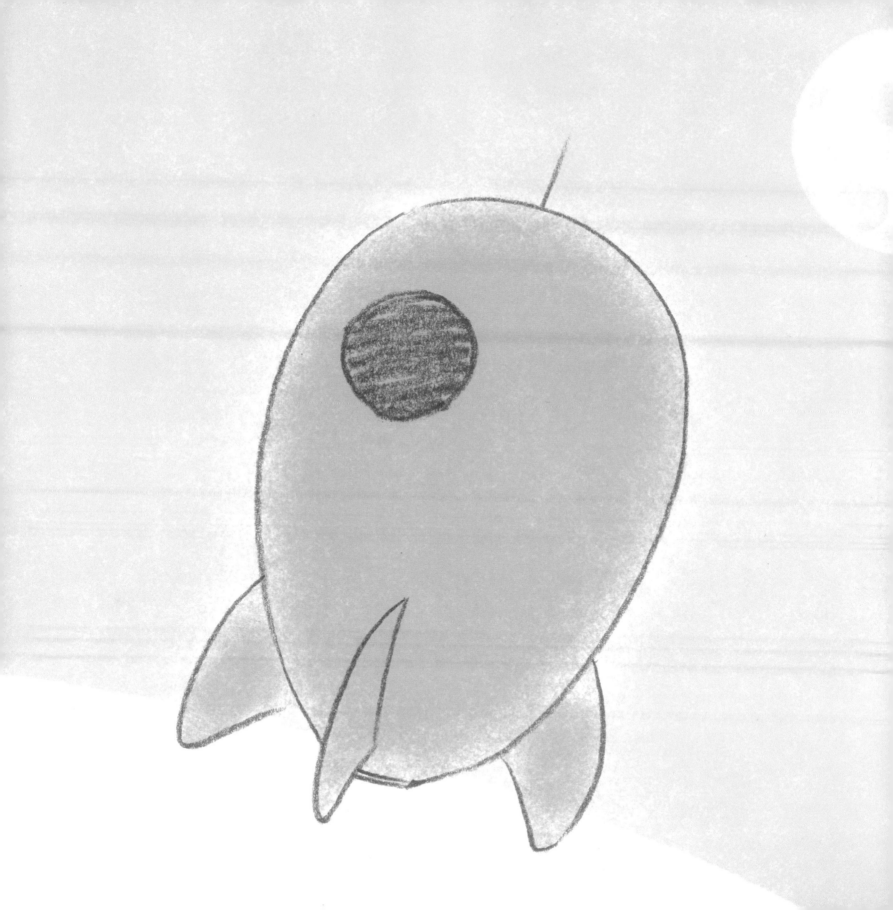

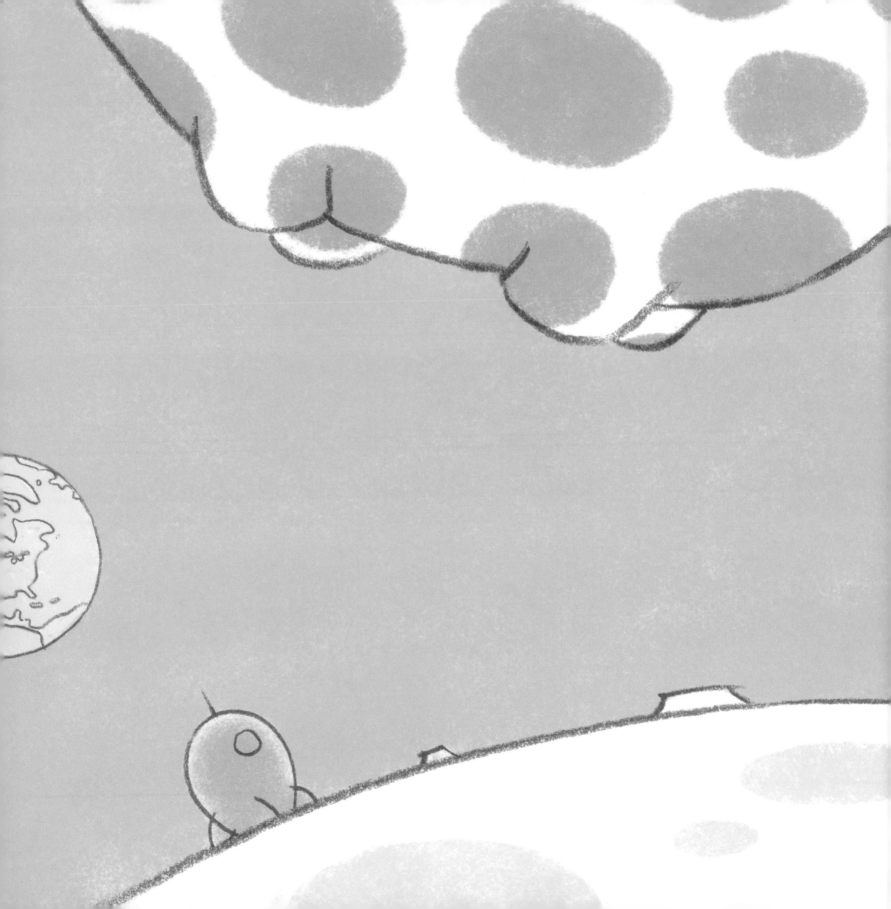

Oliver!

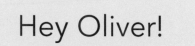

Hey Oliver!

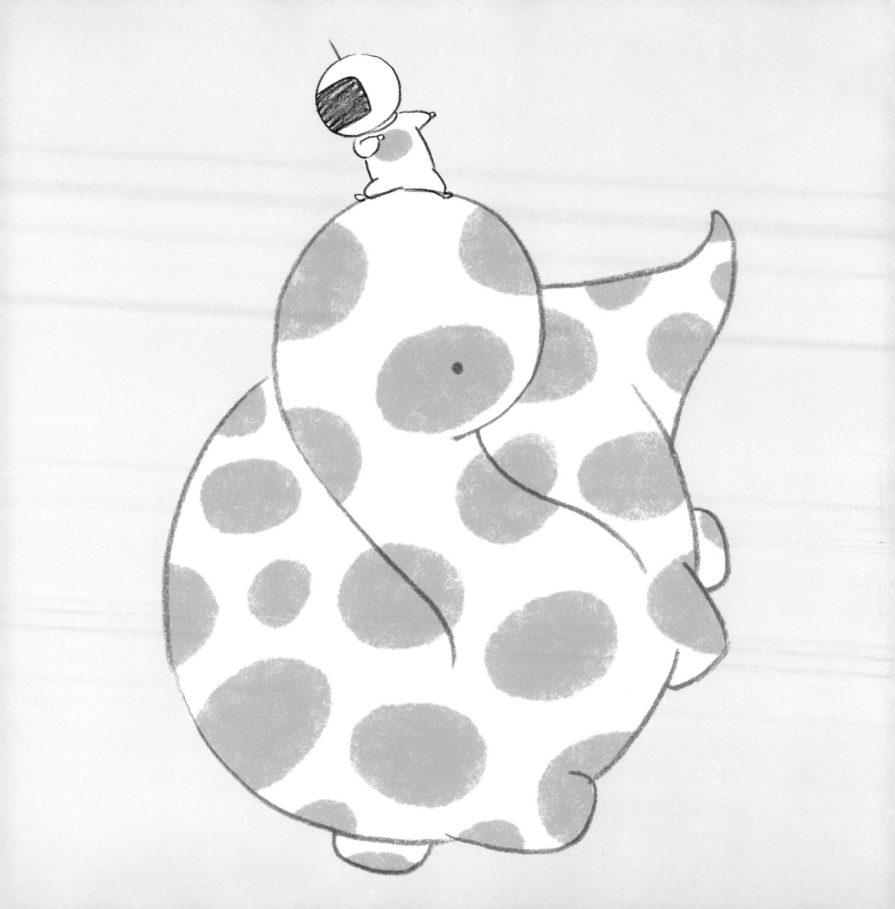

But when Oliver found his rock . . .

Oliver imagined many adventures

with *all* his friends!

First Edition
10 9 8 7 6 5 4 3 2 1
H106-9333-5-14077

Printed in Malaysia
The art is created with pastel pencil and digital color.

Library of Congress Cataloging-in-Publication Data

Schmid, Paul.
  Oliver and his egg / Paul Schmid. — First edition.
      pages cm
  Summary: When Oliver finds an egg, he imagines the amazing adventures
they will have together.
  ISBN-13: 978-1-4231-7573-5
  ISBN-10: 1-4231-7573-5
  [1. Imagination—Fiction. 2. Friendship—Fiction. 3. Eggs—Fiction.] I. Title.
  PZ7.S3492Ole 2014
  [E]—dc23   2013021228

Reinforced binding
Visit www.disneyhyperionbooks.com

CUENTO DE LUZ

To Grima, whose hands cure, caress and cuddle,
but which, when they have to, also drive tractors
that change the world and silence voices.

- Mar Pavón -

To Carmen, my lovely mother, a special woman
with a truly colossal hairdo!

- Nívola Uyá -

A Very, Very Noisy Tractor

Text © Mar Pavón
Illustrations © Nívola Uyá
This edition © 2013 Cuento de Luz SL
Calle Claveles 10 | Urb Monteclaro | Pozuelo de Alarcón | 28223 | Madrid | Spain
www.cuentodeluz.com
Original title in Spanish: Un tractor muy, muy ruidoso
English translation by Jon Brokenbrow

ISBN: 978-84-15619-65-9

Printed by Shanghai Chenxi Printing Co., Ltd. January 2013, print number 1335 – 02

FSC
www.fsc.org
MIX
Paper from
responsible sources
FSC® C007923

A Very, Very Noisy Tractor

Mar Pavón · Nivola Uyá

One day, a lady came chugging down the road on a tractor.
She had an enormous beehive hairdo.
A pizza delivery boy saw her and yelled,
"Ladies with crazy hairdos shouldn't drive tractors!"
The lady didn't hear anything because, as you know, the sound
of a tractor is just like a beehive hairdo ... coLOSSAL!

The tractor chugged down the road with the lady (who, in addition to her beehive hairdo, was wearing a thick pair of eyeglasses) at the wheel.

An old woman who was waiting for the bus saw her and yelled,

"Ladies with glasses shouldn't drive tractors!"

The lady didn't hear anything because, as you know, the sound of a tractor is just like objects on the other side of thick glasses ... enorMOUS!

.

The tractor chugged down the road with the lady (who, in addition to her beehive hairdo and thick glasses, was wearing a bright blue raincoat) at the wheel.

The postman saw her and yelled,

"Ladies with *blue* raincoats shouldn't drive tractors!"

The lady didn't hear anything because, as you know, the sound of a tractor is just like the blue on her raincoat ... **LOUD**!

The tractor chugged down the road with the lady (who, in addition to her beehive hairdo, thick glasses and blue raincoat, was wearing a pair of rubber boots) at the wheel.

A builder saw her and yelled,

"Ladies with rubber boots shouldn't drive tractors!"

The lady didn't hear anything because, as you know, the sound of a tractor is just like a pair of boots sloshing through the mud ... NOISY!

The tractor turned off the road toward a pretty village full of gardens, pine trees, and houses with red tile roofs. By the way, in addition to her beehive hairdo, thick glasses, blue raincoat and rubber boots, the lady driving the tractor had a bright red purse slung over her shoulder.

A little boy saw her and yelled,
"Hi there, lady on the tractor!"
The lady heard him perfectly because, as you know, the sound of a little boy
or little girl yelling is just like the red on her purse ... deafening!

The tractor came to a halt and the lady turned off the motor.

"Hello, young man!" she answered.

"Is that your tractor?" he asked.

"Yes, it is. I use it to plow the fields."

"When I grow up, I'll have one just like it!"

"I'm sure you will," the lady laughed. "I've got to go.

My husband and my daughter are waiting for me to have dinner."

"Does your husband make dinner?" asked the little boy.

"You bet!" said the lady.

"And is he a good cook?"

"Out of this world! He's a great cook. You'll have to stop by

and see for yourself one day, okay?"

"You bet!" said the little boy.

The tractor chugged off again with the lady (who, in addition to her huge beehive hairdo, thick glasses, bright blue raincoat, rubber boots, and bright, bright red purse, now wore a huge smile on her face) at the wheel. Seeing her coming down the road, a man wearing an apron yelled, "What's that lady with the smile doing on a tractor? She should *be* on a carriage!"

The lady didn't hear anything, but she didn't need to, because, as everyone knows, you don't hear the sounds of love with your ears, but with your heart.
In other words, they're like a kiss ... *breathtaking*.

That night, just like every other night, the man with the apron and the lady with the tractor sat down to dinner with their beloved daughter. The dinner, as always, was absolutely delicious. Suddenly, the little girl solemnly announced: "When I grow up, I want to have a tractor and be a FARMER, just like Mom."

Her mother gave her a loving smile, but there was something serious in her eyes. Then she answered:

"Darling, my work is very hard, but if that's what you want, then go for it! I'll only give you one piece of advice: make sure that your tractor is very, very noisy—so noisy that you can't hear the silly things people shout at you."

After dinner, like every other evening, the whole family helped tidy up the table. Then Dad washed the plates, Mom rinsed them and put them away, and the little girl washed her hands and brushed her teeth, put on her pajamas, and read her favorite book until she was ready to sleep.

The tractor stood silently in the garage. A few hours later, when the rooster crowed, its owner would come back for it. She could be wearing her beehive hairdo or her ponytail, thick glasses or contact lenses, a raincoat or a jacket, rubber boots or sneakers, a purse or a backpack—it really didn't matter!

The fact is, no matter what she looked like or what she wore, she was its owner, the lady with the tractor, the only lady farmer in the whole area ... for the time being. And whoever thought it strange that she drove a tractor had only to ask a little boy or a little girl because children always, always see people for who they really are.